# If You're Happy and You Know It!

Adapted by Anna McQuinn

Illustrated by Sophie Fatus

Sung by Susan Reed

**Barefoot Books**

*Step inside a story*

If you're happy and you know it, clap your hands!
If you're happy and you know it, clap your hands!
If you're happy and you know it,
and you really want to show it,
If you're happy and you know it,
clap your hands!

If you're happy and you know it, stamp your feet!
If you're happy and you know it, stamp your feet!

If you're happy and you know it, and you really want to show it,
If you're happy and you know it,
stamp your feet!

If you're happy and you know it, turn around!
If you're happy and you know it, turn around!
If you're happy and you know it, and you really want to show it,
**If you're happy and you know it, turn around!**

If you're happy and you know it, wiggle your hips!
If you're happy and you know it, wiggle your hips!
If you're happy and you know it, and you really want to show it,
If you're happy and you know it, wiggle your hips!

If you're happy and you know it, stretch your arms!
If you're happy and you know it, stretch your arms!
If you're happy and you know it, and you really want to show it,

If you're happy and you know it, stretch your arms!

If you're happy and you know it, pat your head!
If you're happy and you know it, pat your head!
If you're happy and you know it, and you really want to show it,
If you're happy and you know it, pat your head!

If you're happy and you know it, touch your nose!
If you're happy and you know it, touch your nose!
If you're happy and you know it, and you really want to show it,
If you're happy and you know it, touch your nose!

If you're happy and you know it, point your toes!
If you're happy and you know it, point your toes!
If you're happy and you know it, and you really want to show it,
**If you're happy and you know it, point your toes!**

If you're happy and you know it, shout hello!
If you're happy and you know it, shout hello!
If you're happy and you know it, and you really want to show it,
**If you're happy and you know it, shout hello!**

"Merhaba"

"Hau"

"Buen día"

"Selam"

"Hello"

"Hallo"

"Dia duit"

"Salam"

"Kalimera"

"Marhaba"

"G'day"

"Kahé"

"Ayubowan"

"Bom dia"

"Ai"

"Moikka"

"Grüss Gott"

Aurélie
France

Ming Hoa
China (Mandarin)

Lulu
Tanzania

Omar
Pakistan

Konrad
Poland

Parvati
India (Hindi)

Bekele
Ethiopia

Fatima
Malaysia

Sukhindir
India (Punjabi)

Sasha
Russia

Annette
Austria

Oisín
Ireland

Aryana
Afghanistan

Paytah
N. America (Lakot

Zainab
Lebanon

Calida
Greece

Pedro
Portugal

Margriet
The Netherland

Hanako
Japan

Vittorio
Italy

Rabindra
Bangladesh

Amina
Somalia

Ruzivo
Zimbabwe

So-Yee
China    (Cantonese)

Raúl
Spain

Monifa
Nigeria

Asanka

Sri Lanka

Nasih
Eritrea

Hanne
Germany

Mehmet
Turkey

Ben

Canada

Graciela

Mexico

Saimi
Finland

Arapoosh

N. America (Apsáaloke)

Shane

Australia

Kirima

Canada (Inukitut)

# If You're Happy and You Know it!

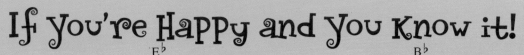

If you're hap—py and you know it clap your hands! If you're

hap—py and you know it clap your hands! If you're hap—py and you know it, and you

real—ly want to show it, if you're hap—py and you know it, clap your hands!

Barefoot Books
2067 Massachusetts Ave
Cambridge, MA 02140

Barefoot Books
29 / 30 Fitzroy Square
London, W1T 6LQ

Adaptation copyright © 2009 by Anna McQuinn
Illustrations copyright © 2009 by Sophie Fatus
Music on the accompanying CD written by Susan Reed;
performed by Susan, Kate and Allison Reed.
Recorded, mixed and mastered by Eric Kilburn at Wellspring Sound, Acton, MA
Animation by Karrot Animation, London
The moral rights of Anna McQuinn and Sophie Fatus have been asserted

First published in Great Britain by Barefoot Books, Ltd
and in the United States of America by Barefoot Books, Inc in 2009
This paperback edition with enhanced CD first published in 2019. All rights reserved
Printed in China by Printplus, Ltd on 100% acid-free paper
Graphic design by Louise Millar, London. Reproduction by B & P International, Hong Kong
This book was typeset in Neu Phollick Alpha and Circus Dog. The illustrations were prepared in acrylics

Paperback with enhanced CD ISBN 978-1-84686-619-7

British Cataloguing-in-Publication Data:
a catalogue record for this book is available from the British Library

Library of Congress Cataloging-in-Publication Data is available under LCCN 2008039827

 Go to *www.barefootbooks.com/ifyourehappy* to access
your audio singalong and video animation online.